Children's Books:

AN ORDINARY PRINCESS

Sally Huss

ISBN: 0982262574
ISBN 13: 9780982262573

A little girl named Laura Sue wished to be a princess. "I wish I were a princess," said Laura Sue. "To be a princess would be priceless."

But Laura Sue was an ordinary little girl, living in an ordinary house with ordinary parents and a very ordinary brother.

"Boy are you ordinary!" said Laura Sue to her brother Henry, who lay sprawled across his bed eating chips and playing video games.

"You're no princess yourself, Laura Sue," snarled Henry.

They glared at each other as they had done so often before.

"Humph!" said Laura Sue, as she walked out of the room.

In the kitchen she found her mother fixing a salad for dinner.

"Mom, I'd like to be a princess," said Laura Sue.

"Sorry," said her mother. "You have to be born a princess. You were born an ordinary girl -- a very pretty one at that -- but definitely not a princess. You are very special to me though," her mother continued, as she gave Laura Sue a hug.

Sadly, Laura Sue left the kitchen and wandered into the family room where her father was reading the evening paper. "Dad, I'd like to be a princess," announced Laura Sue.

"Oh, is it Halloween already?" asked her father.

"No! I mean I want to be a real princess."

"I'm sorry," said her father. "Princesses are daughters of kings and I'm just an ordinary man. We're not a royal family, but you can be my little princess any time you want," he said, as he patted her on the head.

"No, thanks," said Laura Sue. "I want to be a real princess!"

"Oh!" said her father, as she stomped out of the room.

Laura Sue sulked all night long.

Then the next day at school, Laura Sue's spirits brightened as she listened to her teacher Miss Merrifield. "Dear children, you can be anything you want to be -- anything you set your hearts on.

You are so capable, so wonderful, so smart, and so creative.

There is nothing to stop you from being whatever you want to be."

Laura Sue jumped up. "I want to be a princess!" she shouted.

All the children laughed. They thought it absurd for an ordinary girl to want to be a princess.

Miss Merrifield quieted the class and then explained, "What I had in mind, Laura Sue, was -- what would you like to do? For instance, when I was a little girl I wanted to teach and here I am a teacher."

Laura Sue slid down in her seat and covered her head with her sweater as Miss Merrifield continued. "What would the rest of you like to be?"

"A doctor." "A fireman." "A nurse." "A lawyer." "An astronaut." "A movie star." "A pilot." "An artist."

"A policewoman." "A rock star." "A basketball player." These were called out from around the room.

"That's more like it," said Miss Merrifield smiling.

Laura Sue continued to hide until she got home and even then she slunk around the house moping. "What's wrong?" her mother asked.

"Nothing."

"Got a problem?" asked her dad.

"Nope."

At the dinner table that evening, her brother teased her, "She's just upset because she can't be a princess!"

"I can be anything I want to be," said Laura Sue, as she left the table. "Miss Merrifield said so!"

"But not a princess!" her brother shouted after her. He had obviously heard what had happened in her class that day.

Laura Sue went to her room, flopped down on her bed, hiding her face in her pillow, and fell asleep.

That night, a beautiful, golden angel came to her in a dream.

The angel asked, "What is it you wish, Laura Sue?"

"I wish I were a princess with all my heart. To be a princess would be priceless."

"Well, you can't be a royal princess with castles and crowns and gowns. But you can be an ordinary princess and gain the appreciation and respect of all those around you, which is worth more than all the gold in any kingdom."

"Oh my," sighed Laura Sue, with her hand over her heart.

"How do I do that?"

"Like Miss Merrifield said," the angel explained, "it's what you do that makes you what you are. To be a princess you must act like a princess. You must be kind and happy and helpful and never, never complain."

"Oh, I can do that," said Laura Sue. "Kind and happy and helpful and never, never complain," repeated Laura Sue.

"Very good," said the angel, as she kissed Laura Sue goodbye.

The next day, Laura Sue put into practice her new vocation -- princess-ship. She helped her brother take his model airplane to school for show-and-tell. "That is really kind of you. Thanks, Laura Sue," said Henry.

She shared her spelling paper with its "100%" mark on it with her father, and that made him very happy. "You would be a jewel in the crown of any king," he said sweetly.

She helped her mother after dinner by clearing the table and emptying the trash. "You're no ordinary girl, Laura Sue," said her mother proudly.

And, she did her homework that took over an hour and never once complained about it. "Good girl, Laura Sue," said her mother, as she peeked in on her. "What a princess," she said under her breath.

Laura Sue heard her mother and smiled. Being a princess <u>is</u> priceless, thought Laura Sue. Being a princess doesn't have to do with gold or crowns or gowns. It has to do with being kind and happy and helpful, and never, never complaining.

Now that Laura Sue knew what she was -- an Ordinary

Princess -- being herself suited her just fine!

The end, but not the end of being kind and happy and helpful.

You too can be an ordinary princess or prince by remembering to be kind and happy and helpful, and by never complaining.

At the end of this book you will find a Certificate of Merit that may be issued to any child who promises to honor the requirements stated in the Certificate. This fine Certificate will easily fit into a 5"x7" frame, and happily suit any child who receives it!

Here are a few Sally Huss books you might enjoy. They may be found on Amazon as e-books and as soft cover books.

http://amzn.to/20VJeP5

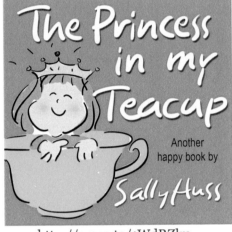

http://amzn.to/1WdRZlm

http://amzn.to/1Pop8Xa

http://amzn.to/1WdSa04

Sally writes new books all the time. If you would like to be alerted when one of her new books becomes available or when one of her books is offered FREE on Amazon, sign up here: http://www.sallyhuss.com/kids-books.html.

If you liked AN ORDINARY PRINCESS, please be kind enough to post a short review on Amazon by using this URL: http://amzn.com/B00N1IR0IS.

For more information on books by Sally Huss, you may go to http://amzn.to/1FoQtbk.

About the Author/Illustrator

Sally Huss

"Bright and happy," "light and whimsical" have been the catch phrases attached to the writings and art of Sally Huss for over 30 years. Sweet images dance across all of Sally's creations, whether in the form of children's books, paintings, wallpaper, ceramics, baby bibs, purses, clothing, or her King Features syndicated newspaper panel "Happy Musings."

Sally creates children's books to uplift the lives of children and hopes you will join her in this effort by helping spread her happy messages.

Sally is a graduate of USC with a degree in Fine Art and through the years has had 26 of her own licensed art galleries throughout the world.

This certificate may be cut out, framed, and presented to any child who practices being an Ordinary Princess/Prince.

Certificate of Merit

(Name)

The child named above is awarded this Certificate of Merit for becoming an Ordinary Princess or Prince by being:

*Kind to everyone
*Happy at all times
*Helpful whenever possible
*Appreciative, and never complaining

Presented by: _____   Date: _____

40333527R00024

Made in the USA
San Bernardino, CA
16 October 2016